MAX & MO's
100th Day of School!

For Alisa Soriano—Educator Extraordinaire:
with thanks for her 100+ ideas
—Patricia Lakin

For Beau
—Priscilla Lamont

SIMON SPOTLIGHT
An imprint of Simon & Schuster Children's Publishing Division
1230 Avenue of the Americas, New York, New York 10020
This Simon Spotlight edition November 2020
Text copyright © 2020 by Patricia Lakin
Illustrations copyright © 2020 by Brian Floca
All rights reserved, including the right of reproduction
in whole or in part in any form.
SIMON SPOTLIGHT, READY-TO-READ, and colophon are
registered trademarks of Simon & Schuster, Inc.
For information about special discounts for bulk purchases, please
contact Simon & Schuster Special Sales at 1-866-506-1949
or business@simonandschuster.com.
Manufactured in the United States of America 0920 LAK
2 4 6 8 10 9 7 5 3 1
This book has been cataloged with the Library of Congress.
ISBN 978-1-5344-6326-4 (hc)
ISBN 978-1-5344-6325-7 (pbk)
ISBN 978-1-5344-6327-1 (eBook)

MAX & MO's
100th Day of School!

By Patricia Lakin
Illustrated by Priscilla Lamont
in the style of Brian Floca

Ready-to-Read

Simon Spotlight
New York   London   Toronto   Sydney   New Delhi

Max and Mo were
best friends.

They lived in a cozy cage
in the art room at school.

Max liked to make things.
Mo liked to read things.
"Look! The big ones are
making crowns," said Max.

"But why do their crowns say '100'?" Max asked.

Mo read the sign. "They are getting ready for their 100th day of school party."

"That means it is our
100th day of school too.
And we love parties!" Mo said.

Max and Mo waited for the
big ones to leave.

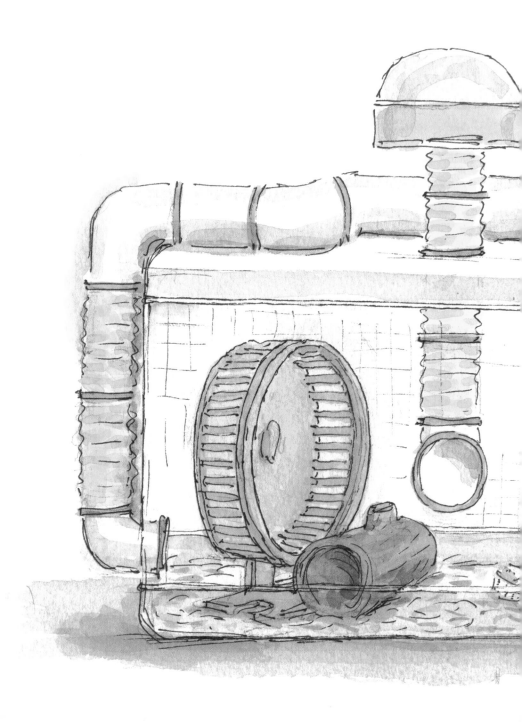

"We can use our chain
to climb out and down,"
said Max.
"One-two-three!
Down we jump!"

"What can we make?"
asked Mo.

Max scratched his chin.
"We can make crowns too.
This shows us what to do."

Max and Mo proudly
wore their crowns.
"We are counting kings!"
Mo said.

Max scratched his chin.
"We need to count to 100.
What should we count?"

"Beads," said Mo.

"We can make a necklace!"

Oops! Max tripped.

Mo slipped.

Beads flipped . . .

. . . right into a bead bin.
Max scratched his chin.
"Now what?"

"We are counting kings.
We can count out 100 beads!"
said Mo.

"That is a lot of counting,"
said Max.

"This sign gives us a hint.
We can count by tens,"
Mo said.

Make counting to 100 easy.
Make 10 piles of 10.

10, 20, 30,
40, 50, 60
70, 80, 90,
100!

"Ten, twenty, thirty,
forty, fifty, sixty,
seventy, eighty, ninety . . ."

"100!" they cheered.
They put the beads
on a string.

"That was fun!
We can make another one!"

They hung a necklace
on the wall.

"One-two-three!
Up we jump!"
Max and Mo climbed
up and in.

They got ready
for the party just in time!
The big ones came back.

"It is time for our party!"
the big ones cheered.

"Happy 100th
day of school,
Max and Mo!"

Want to make a necklace
using 100 objects?
Here is what you will need:

1. A grown-up's help
2. A string or a shoelace

3. Paper clips, beads, or pieces
   of dry pasta (with holes
   in them)

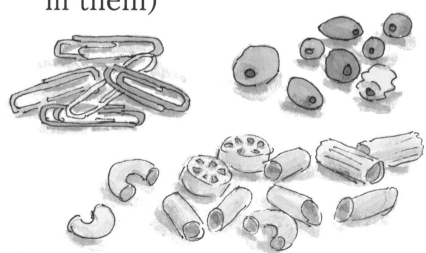

Here is what to do:

1. Count out 100 items.

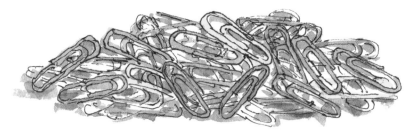

2. String or clip them together.

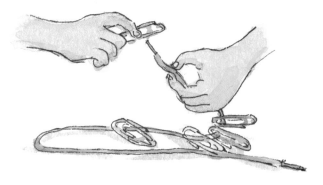

3. Tie the string or shoelace.

4. Proudly wear your necklace!

Which bag holds 100 items? Test a grown-up on their counting skills!

Here is what you will need:
1. Fill one with 100 pennies.
2. Fill another with 100 paper clips. Ask, "Which bag has the most objects?" (Which bag did they pick? Just because one bag looks bigger than the other doesn't mean it holds more objects!)